D1276841

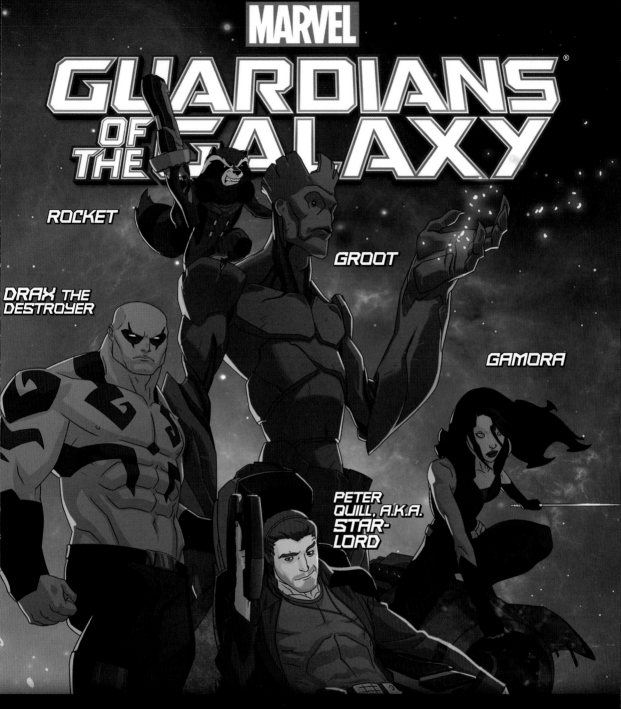

MARVEL
GUARDIANS OF THE GALAXY

ROCKET

GROOT

DRAX THE DESTROYER

GAMORA

PETER QUILL, A.K.A. STAR-LORD

PREVIOUSLY:
The Guardians came into possession of a mysterious
Spartaxan cube that holds a map to an object of immense
power called the Cosmic Seed. Half Spartaxan, Star-Lord is
the only one able to access the map. Now the Guardians must
find the Seed before Thanos does.

Volume 9: We Are Family
BASED ON THE DISNEY XD ANIMATED TV SERIES

Written by STEVE MELCHING   Directed by JAMES YANG
Animation Art Produced by MARVEL ANIMATION STUDIOS   Adapted by JOE CARAMAGNA

Special Thanks to
HANNAH MACDONALD
& PRODUCT FACTORY

MARK BASSO editor
AXEL ALONSO editor in chief
DAN BUCKLEY publisher

MARK PANICCIA senior editor
JOE QUESADA chief creative officer
ALAN FINE executive producer

ABDOBOOKS.COM

Reinforced library bound edition published in 2020 by Spotlight,
a division of ABDO, PO Box 398166, Minneapolis, Minnesota 55439.
Spotlight produces high-quality reinforced library bound editions for
schools and libraries. Published by agreement with Marvel Characters, Inc.

Printed in the United States of America, North Mankato, Minnesota.
042019
092019

THIS BOOK CONTAINS
RECYCLED MATERIALS

marvelkids.com
© 2020 MARVEL

Library of Congress Control Number: 2018965975

Publisher's Cataloging-in-Publication Data

Names: Caramagna, Joe; Melching, Steven, authors. | Marvel Animation Studios,
     illustrator.
Title: We are family / by Joe Caramagna ; Steven Melching; illustrated by Marvel
     Animation Studios.
Description: Minneapolis, Minnesota : Spotlight, 2020. | Series: Guardians of the
     Galaxy set 3 ; volume 9
Summary: When Rocket is abducted and taken back to his home planet Half World,
     the Guardians rush to the planet where they find Rocket caught up in a
     revolution of evolved former test subject animals.
Identifiers: ISBN 9781532143601 (lib. bdg.)
Subjects: LCSH: Guardians of the Galaxy (Fictitious characters)--Juvenile fiction. |
     Superheroes--Juvenile fiction. | Space rescue operations--Juvenile fiction. |
     Graphic novels--Juvenile fiction. | Rocket Raccoon (Fictitious character)--
     Juvenile fiction. | Space--Juvenile fiction. | Comic books, strips, etc--Juvenile
     fiction.
Classification: DDC 741.5--dc23

Spotlight

A Division of ABDO
abdobooks.com

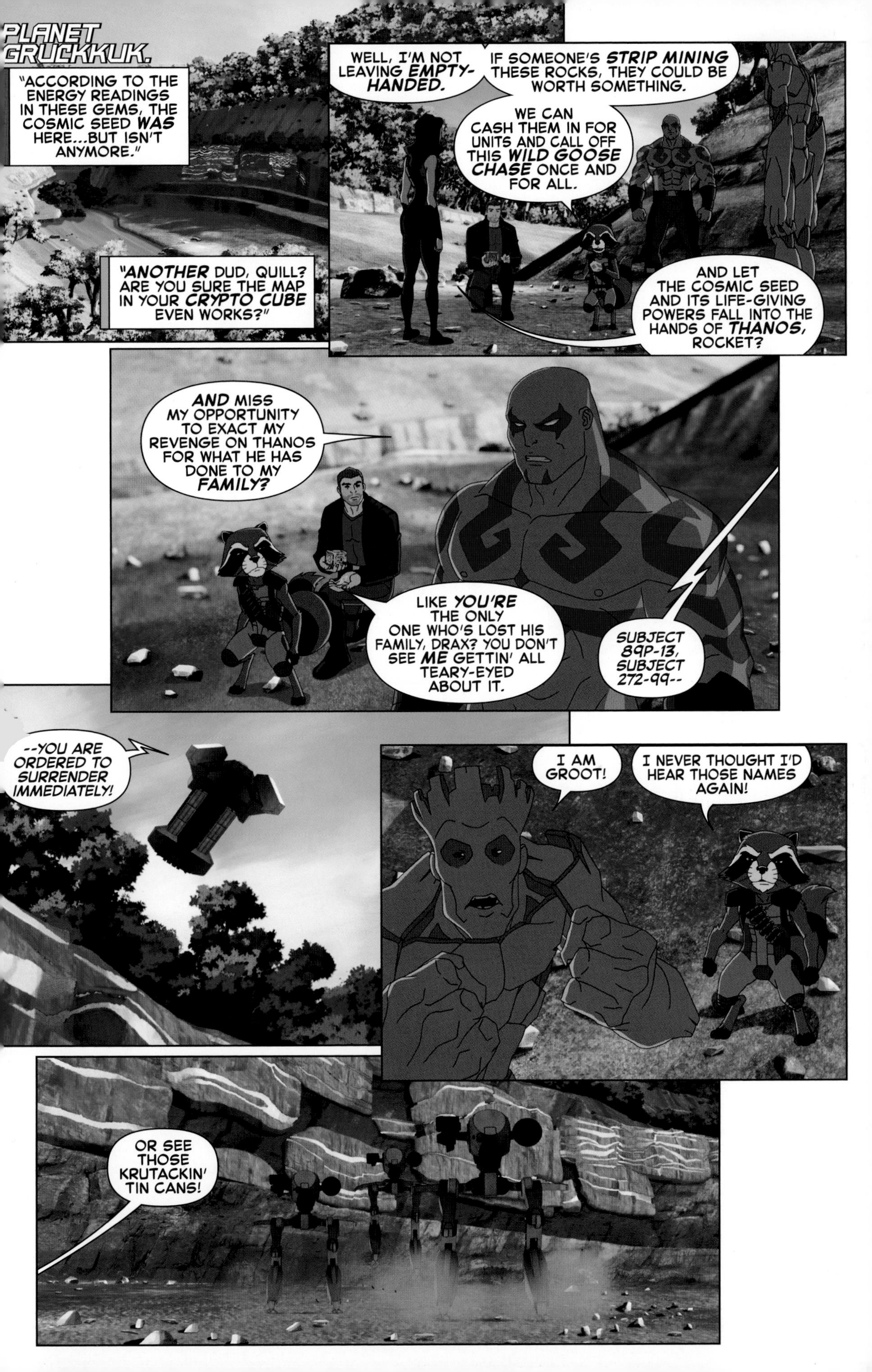
PLANET GRUCKKUK.
"ACCORDING TO THE ENERGY READINGS IN THESE GEMS, THE COSMIC SEED WAS HERE...BUT ISN'T ANYMORE."
"ANOTHER DUD, QUILL? ARE YOU SURE THE MAP IN YOUR CRYPTO CUBE EVEN WORKS?"
WELL, I'M NOT LEAVING EMPTY-HANDED.
IF SOMEONE'S STRIP MINING THESE ROCKS, THEY COULD BE WORTH SOMETHING.
WE CAN CASH THEM IN FOR UNITS AND CALL OFF THIS WILD GOOSE CHASE ONCE AND FOR ALL.
AND LET THE COSMIC SEED AND ITS LIFE-GIVING POWERS FALL INTO THE HANDS OF THANOS, ROCKET?
AND MISS MY OPPORTUNITY TO EXACT MY REVENGE ON THANOS FOR WHAT HE HAS DONE TO MY FAMILY?
LIKE YOU'RE THE ONLY ONE WHO'S LOST HIS FAMILY, DRAX? YOU DON'T SEE ME GETTIN' ALL TEARY-EYED ABOUT IT.
SUBJECT 89P-13, SUBJECT 272-99--
--YOU ARE ORDERED TO SURRENDER IMMEDIATELY!
I AM GROOT!
I NEVER THOUGHT I'D HEAR THOSE NAMES AGAIN!
OR SEE THOSE KRUTACKIN' TIN CANS!

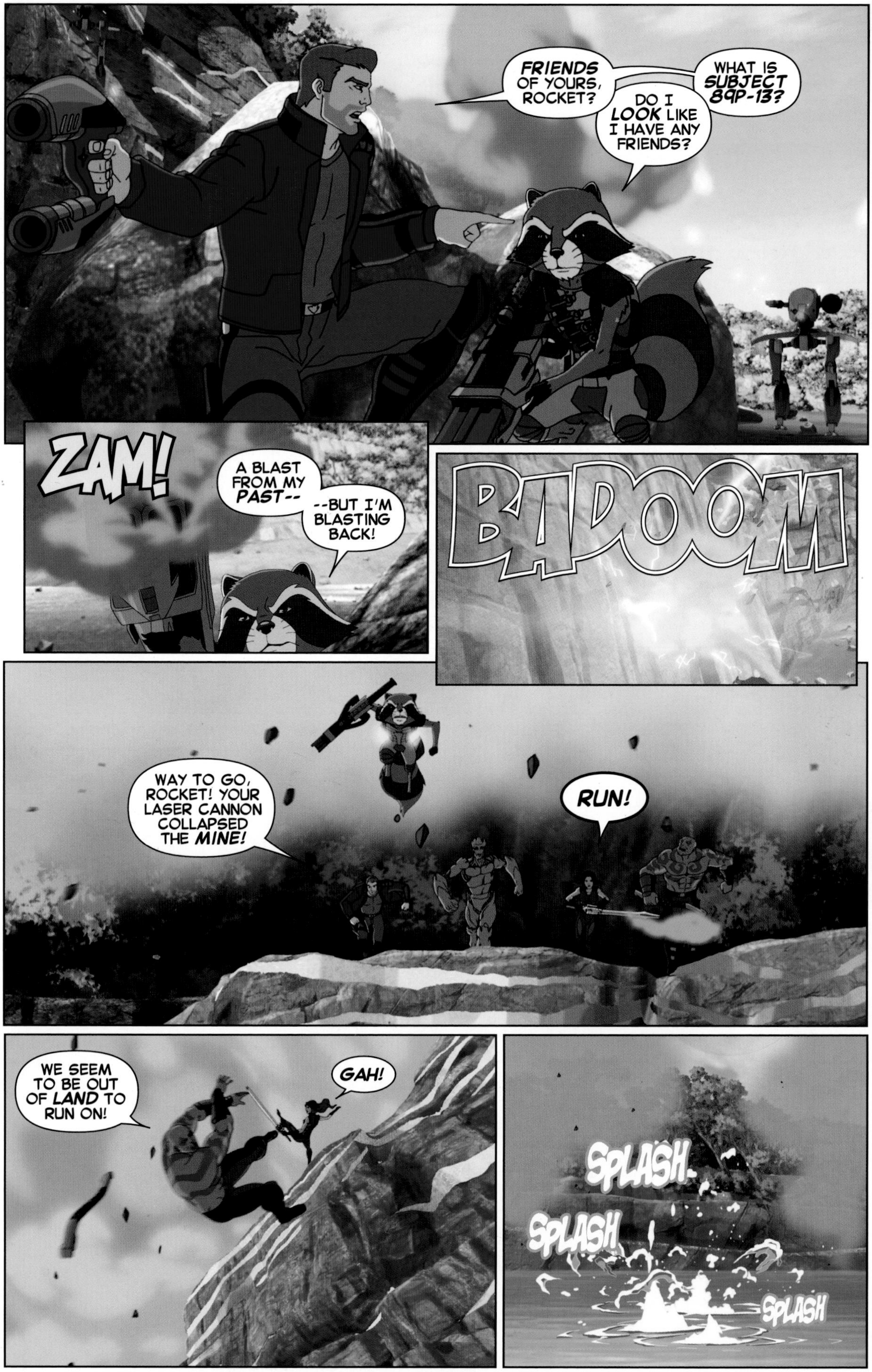
FRIENDS OF YOURS, ROCKET?
WHAT IS SUBJECT 89P-13?
DO I LOOK LIKE I HAVE ANY FRIENDS?
ZAM!
A BLAST FROM MY PAST--
--BUT I'M BLASTING BACK!
BADOOM
WAY TO GO, ROCKET! YOUR LASER CANNON COLLAPSED THE MINE!
RUN!
WE SEEM TO BE OUT OF LAND TO RUN ON!
GAH!
SPLASH
SPLASH
SPLASH

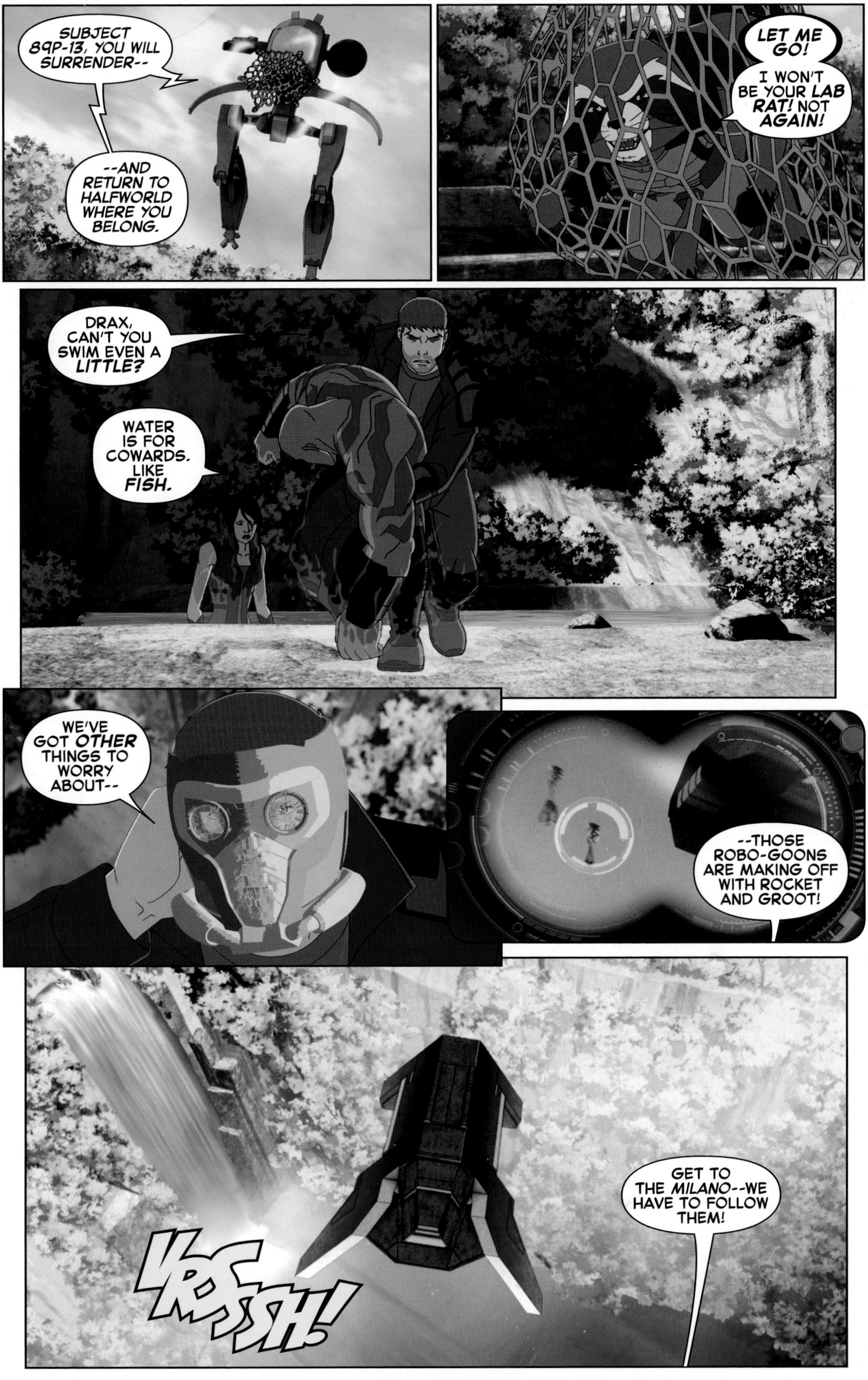
SUBJECT 89P-13, YOU WILL SURRENDER--
--AND RETURN TO HALFWORLD WHERE YOU BELONG.
LET ME GO!
I WON'T BE YOUR LAB RAT! NOT AGAIN!
DRAX, CAN'T YOU SWIM EVEN A LITTLE?
WATER IS FOR COWARDS. LIKE FISH.
WE'VE GOT OTHER THINGS TO WORRY ABOUT--
--THOSE ROBO-GOONS ARE MAKING OFF WITH ROCKET AND GROOT!
GET TO THE MILANO--WE HAVE TO FOLLOW THEM!
VROSSH!

"SUBJECT 89P-13, SUBJECT 272-99-- WE HAVE BEEN TRACKING YOU FOR SOME TIME VIA YOUR CYBERNETIC IMPLANTS."

"YOU HAVE INFORMATION WE REQUIRE."

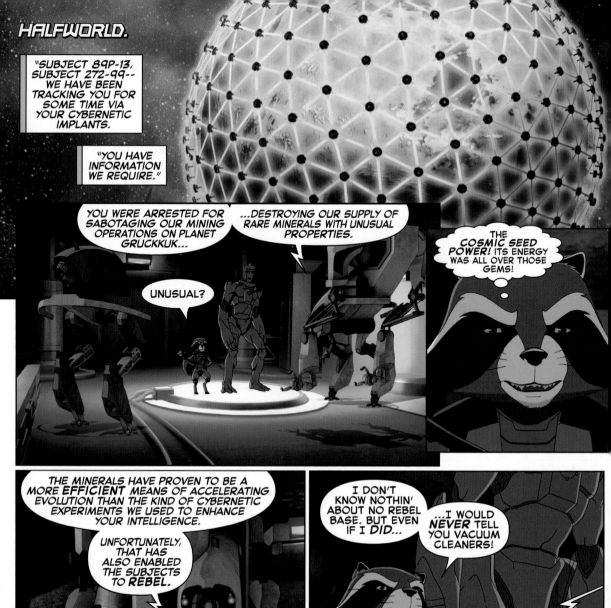

YOU WERE ARRESTED FOR SABOTAGING OUR MINING OPERATIONS ON PLANET GRUCKKUK...

...DESTROYING OUR SUPPLY OF RARE MINERALS WITH UNUSUAL PROPERTIES.

UNUSUAL?

THE COSMIC SEED POWER! ITS ENERGY WAS ALL OVER THOSE GEMS!

THE MINERALS HAVE PROVEN TO BE A MORE EFFICIENT MEANS OF ACCELERATING EVOLUTION THAN THE KIND OF CYBERNETIC EXPERIMENTS WE USED TO ENHANCE YOUR INTELLIGENCE.

UNFORTUNATELY, THAT HAS ALSO ENABLED THE SUBJECTS TO REBEL.

YOU WILL TELL ME THE LOCATION OF THEIR REBEL BASE OR SUFFER THE CONSEQUENCES.

I DON'T KNOW NOTHIN' ABOUT NO REBEL BASE. BUT EVEN IF I DID...

...I WOULD NEVER TELL YOU VACUUM CLEANERS!

WE ANTICIPATED THAT YOU WOULD FEEL THAT WAY...

...SO WE PREPARED A CONTINGENCY PLAN.

JEN?

MOM?!

Y-YOU'RE STILL HERE...AND YOU'RE WALKING UPRIGHT NOW?

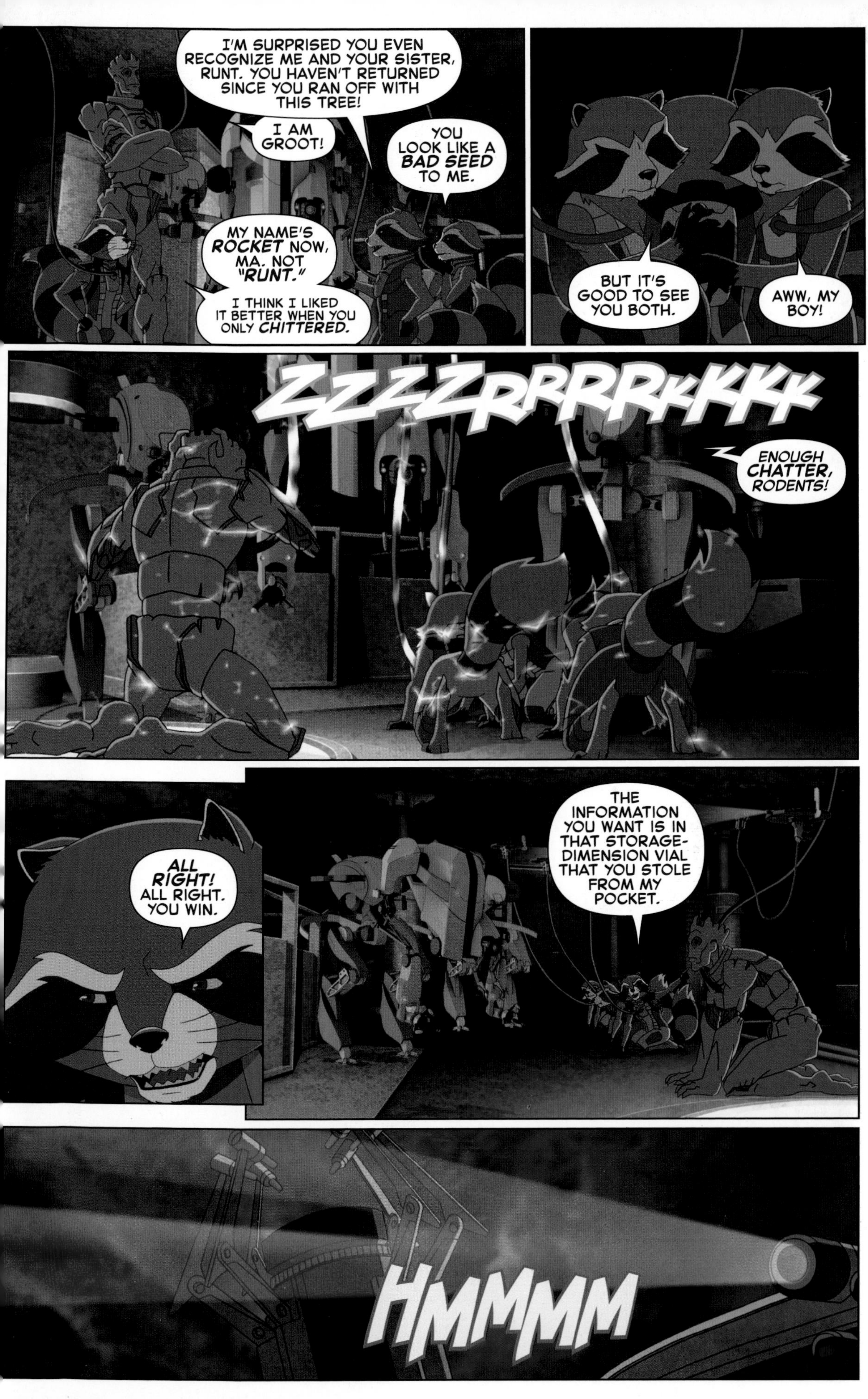
I'M SURPRISED YOU EVEN RECOGNIZE ME AND YOUR SISTER, RUNT. YOU HAVEN'T RETURNED SINCE YOU RAN OFF WITH THIS TREE!
I AM GROOT!
YOU LOOK LIKE A BAD SEED TO ME.
MY NAME'S ROCKET NOW, MA. NOT "RUNT."
I THINK I LIKED IT BETTER WHEN YOU ONLY CHITTERED.
BUT IT'S GOOD TO SEE YOU BOTH.
AWW, MY BOY!
ZZZZRRRRKKK
ENOUGH CHATTER, RODENTS!
ALL RIGHT! ALL RIGHT. YOU WIN.
THE INFORMATION YOU WANT IS IN THAT STORAGE-DIMENSION VIAL THAT YOU STOLE FROM MY POCKET.
HMMMM

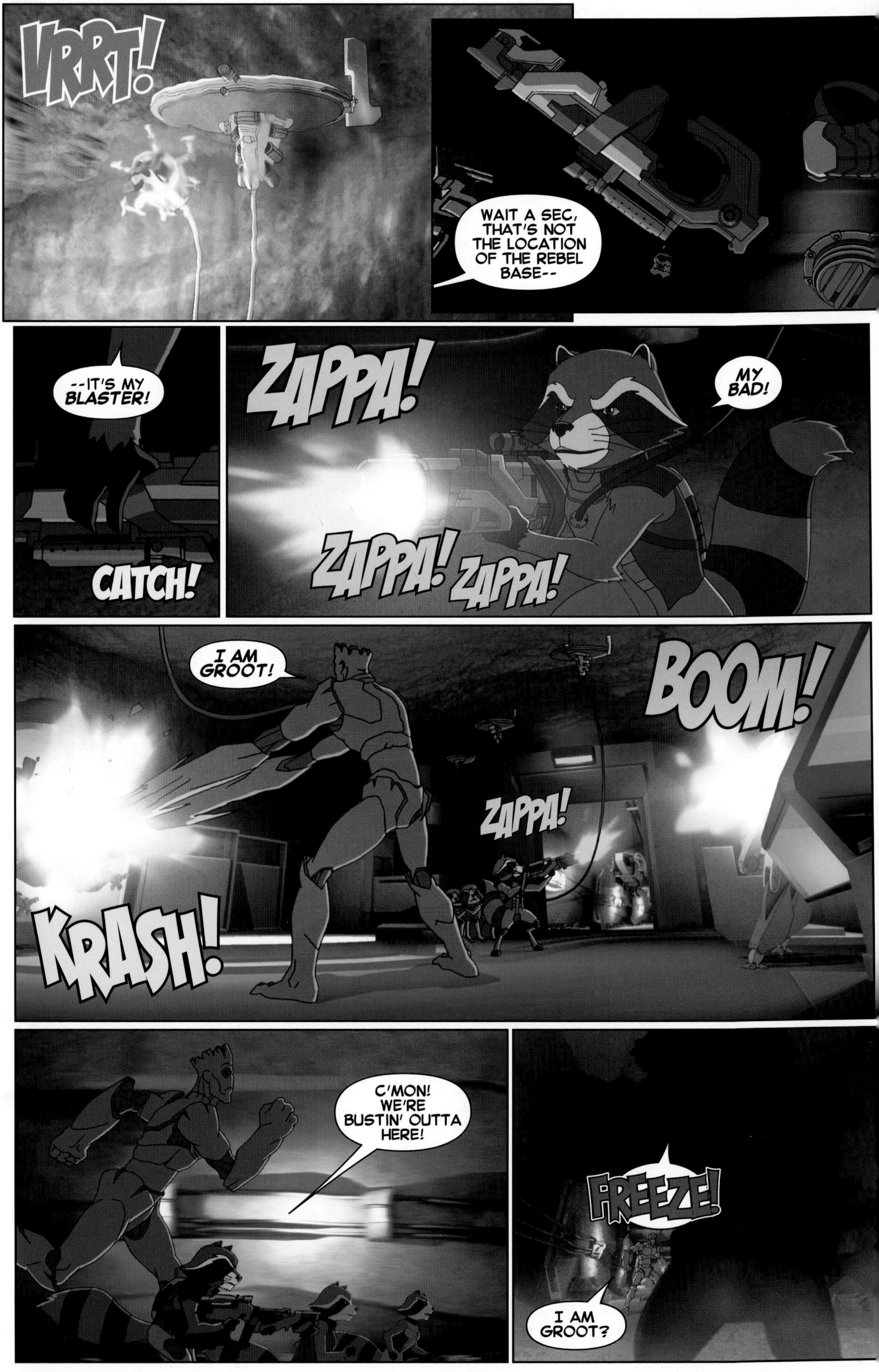
VRRT!
WAIT A SEC, THAT'S NOT THE LOCATION OF THE REBEL BASE--
--IT'S MY BLASTER!
CATCH!
ZAPPA!
MY BAD!
ZAPPA! ZAPPA!
I AM GROOT!
BOOM!
ZAPPA!
KRASH!
C'MON! WE'RE BUSTIN' OUTTA HERE!
FREEZE!
I AM GROOT?

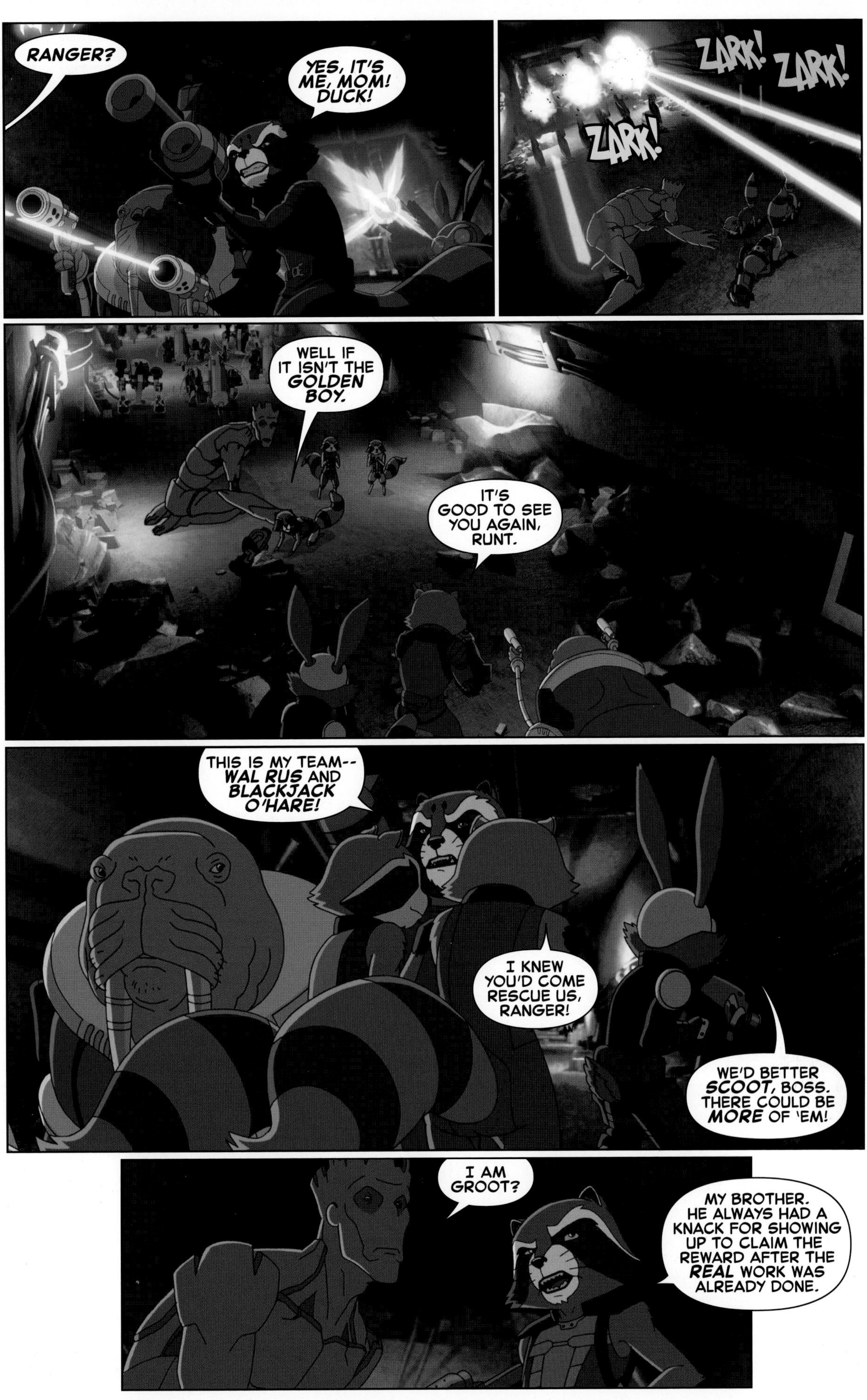
RANGER?
YES, IT'S ME, MOM! DUCK!
ZARK! ZARK!
ZARK!
WELL IF IT ISN'T THE GOLDEN BOY.
IT'S GOOD TO SEE YOU AGAIN, RUNT.
THIS IS MY TEAM-- WAL RUS AND BLACKJACK O'HARE!
I KNEW YOU'D COME RESCUE US, RANGER!
WE'D BETTER SCOOT, BOSS. THERE COULD BE MORE OF 'EM!
I AM GROOT?
MY BROTHER. HE ALWAYS HAD A KNACK FOR SHOWING UP TO CLAIM THE REWARD AFTER THE REAL WORK WAS ALREADY DONE.

LATER.

THIS IS YOUR REBEL BASE?

THIS IS THE PLACE WHERE THEY *EXPERIMENTED* ON ME!

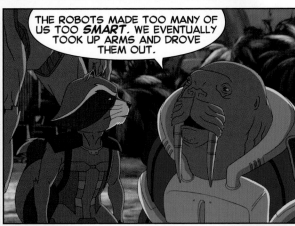

THE ROBOTS MADE TOO MANY OF US TOO *SMART.* WE EVENTUALLY TOOK UP ARMS AND DROVE THEM OUT.

I AM... GROOT?

SUSPICIOUS? SEEMS LIKE *JUSTICE* TO ME!

LET'S CALL THE OTHER GUARDIANS TO PICK US UP SO WE CAN *DITCH* THIS JOINT-- FOR *GOOD* THIS TIME!

FORGET IT, BRO. ALL COMMUNICATION SIGNALS BOUNCE OFF THE *GALACIAN WALL* THE ROBOTS BUILT AROUND THE PLANET.

WHAT'S YOUR HURRY, ANYWAY?

NOW THAT WE'RE *REUNITED...*

...LET'S SAVOR THE MOMENT.

WOULD IT KILL YA TO SMILE, RUNT?

SO OUR CONQUERING HEROES HAVE ARRIVED!

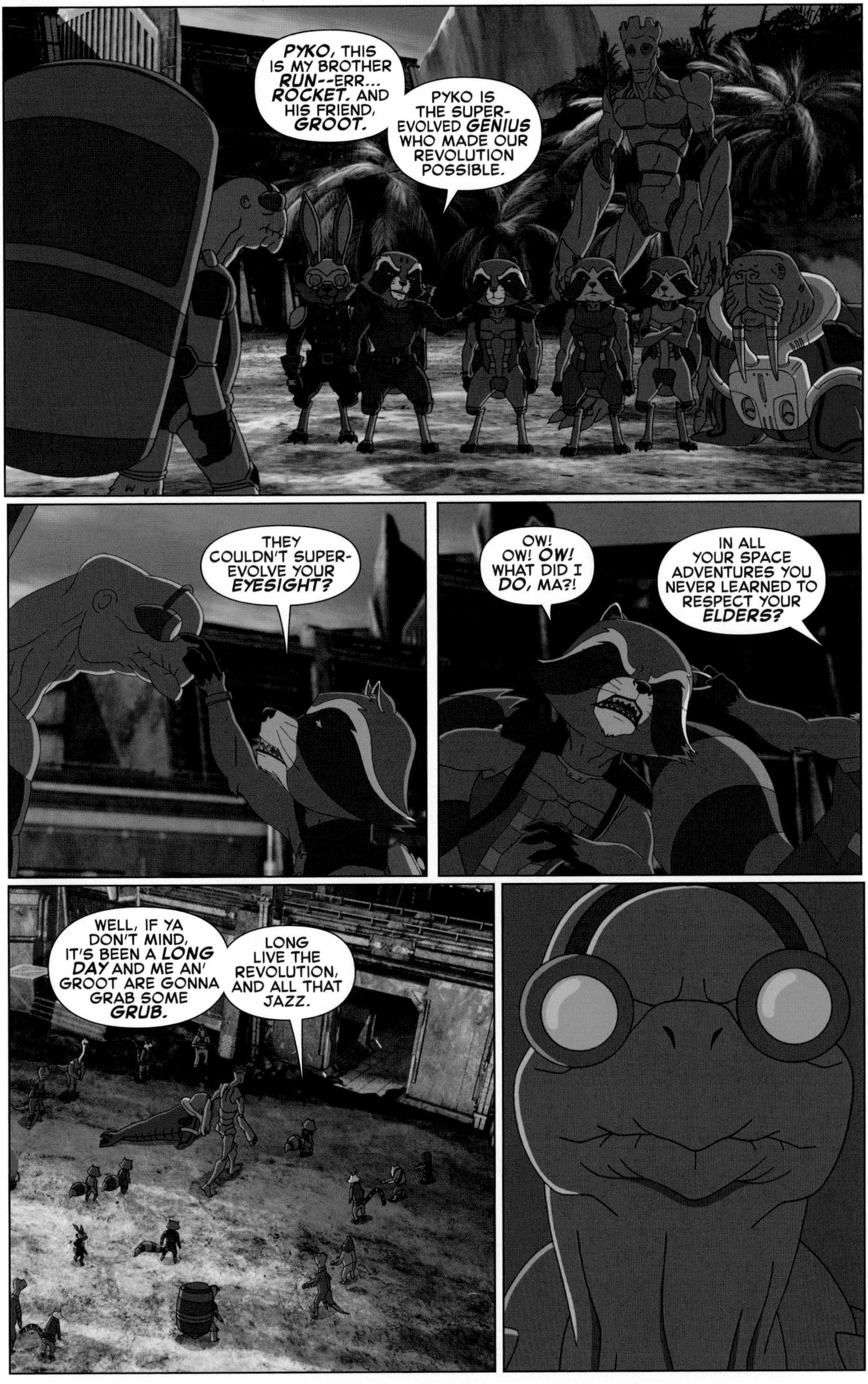
PYKO, THIS IS MY BROTHER RUN--ERR... ROCKET. AND HIS FRIEND, GROOT.
PYKO IS THE SUPER-EVOLVED GENIUS WHO MADE OUR REVOLUTION POSSIBLE.
THEY COULDN'T SUPER-EVOLVE YOUR EYESIGHT?
OW! OW! OW! WHAT DID I DO, MA?!
IN ALL YOUR SPACE ADVENTURES YOU NEVER LEARNED TO RESPECT YOUR ELDERS?
WELL, IF YA DON'T MIND, IT'S BEEN A LONG DAY AND ME AN' GROOT ARE GONNA GRAB SOME GRUB.
LONG LIVE THE REVOLUTION, AND ALL THAT JAZZ.

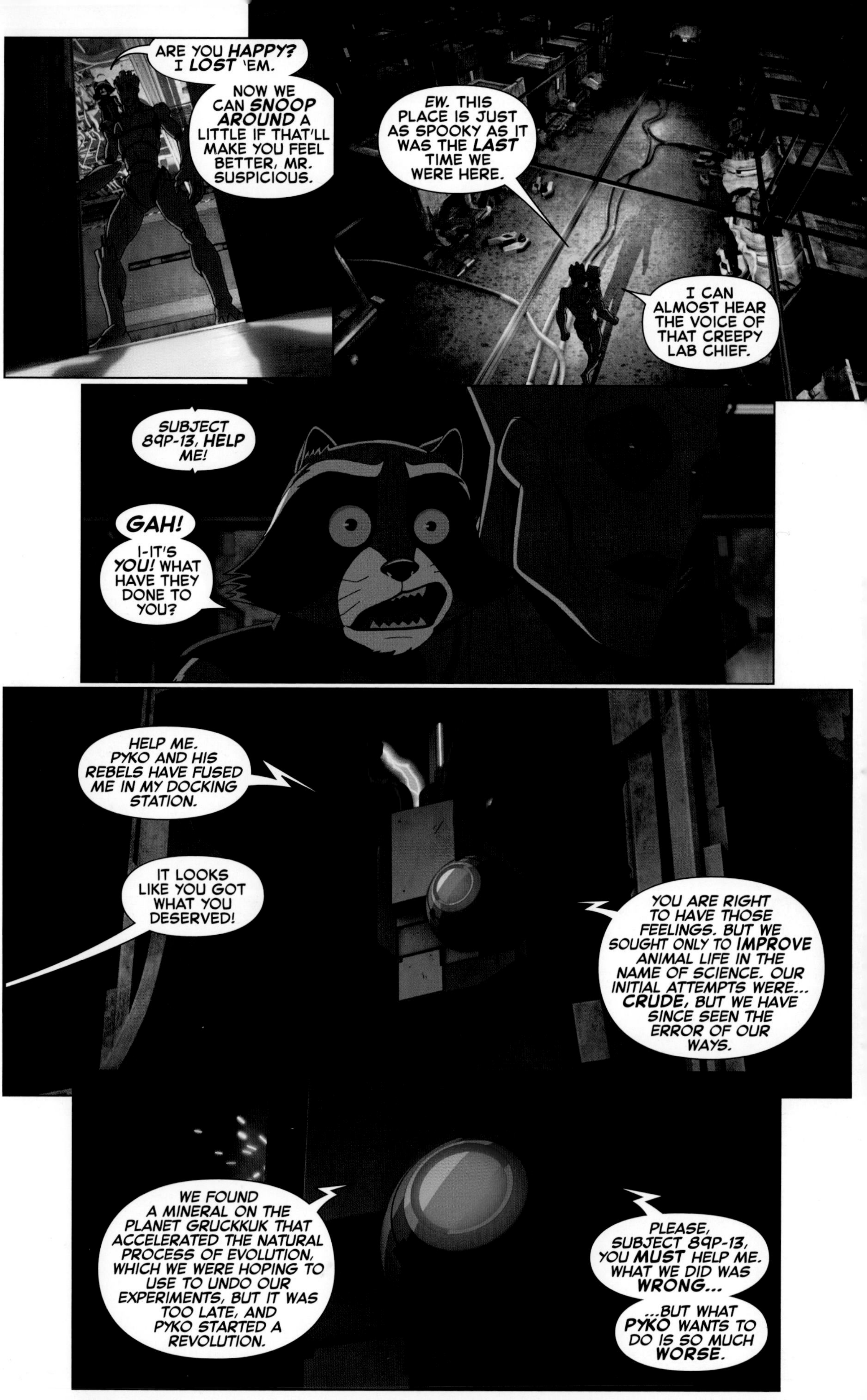
ARE YOU HAPPY? I LOST 'EM.
NOW WE CAN SNOOP AROUND A LITTLE IF THAT'LL MAKE YOU FEEL BETTER, MR. SUSPICIOUS.
EW. THIS PLACE IS JUST AS SPOOKY AS IT WAS THE LAST TIME WE WERE HERE.
I CAN ALMOST HEAR THE VOICE OF THAT CREEPY LAB CHIEF.
SUBJECT 89P-13, HELP ME!
GAH!
I-IT'S YOU! WHAT HAVE THEY DONE TO YOU?
HELP ME. PYKO AND HIS REBELS HAVE FUSED ME IN MY DOCKING STATION.
IT LOOKS LIKE YOU GOT WHAT YOU DESERVED!
YOU ARE RIGHT TO HAVE THOSE FEELINGS. BUT WE SOUGHT ONLY TO IMPROVE ANIMAL LIFE IN THE NAME OF SCIENCE. OUR INITIAL ATTEMPTS WERE... CRUDE, BUT WE HAVE SINCE SEEN THE ERROR OF OUR WAYS.
WE FOUND A MINERAL ON THE PLANET GRUCKKUK THAT ACCELERATED THE NATURAL PROCESS OF EVOLUTION, WHICH WE WERE HOPING TO USE TO UNDO OUR EXPERIMENTS, BUT IT WAS TOO LATE, AND PYKO STARTED A REVOLUTION.
PLEASE, SUBJECT 89P-13, YOU MUST HELP ME. WHAT WE DID WAS WRONG...
...BUT WHAT PYKO WANTS TO DO IS SO MUCH WORSE.

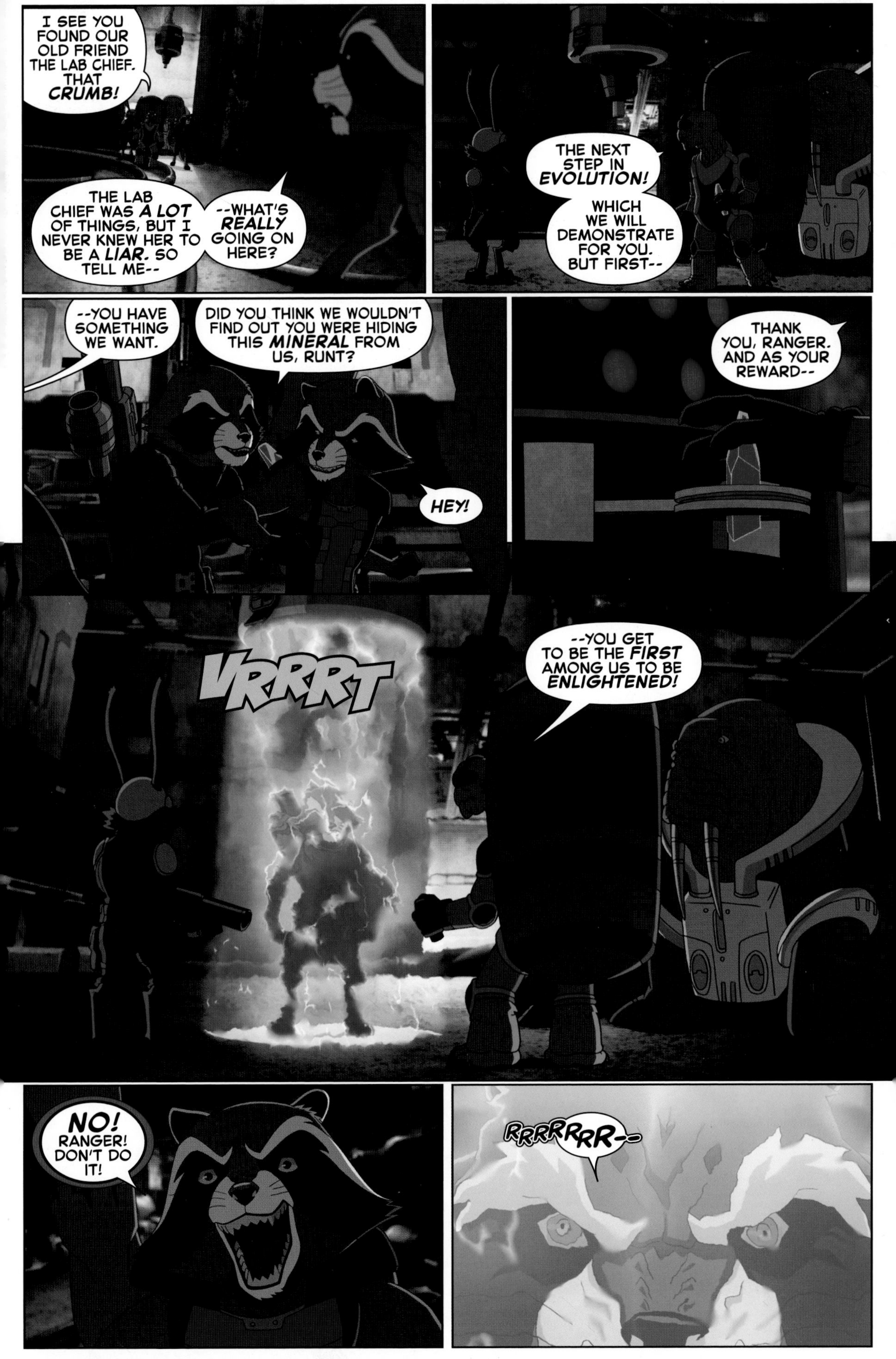
I SEE YOU FOUND OUR OLD FRIEND THE LAB CHIEF. THAT CRUMB!
THE LAB CHIEF WAS A LOT OF THINGS, BUT I NEVER KNEW HER TO BE A LIAR. SO TELL ME--
--WHAT'S REALLY GOING ON HERE?
THE NEXT STEP IN EVOLUTION!
WHICH WE WILL DEMONSTRATE FOR YOU. BUT FIRST--
--YOU HAVE SOMETHING WE WANT.
DID YOU THINK WE WOULDN'T FIND OUT YOU WERE HIDING THIS MINERAL FROM US, RUNT?
HEY!
THANK YOU, RANGER. AND AS YOUR REWARD--
VRRRT
--YOU GET TO BE THE FIRST AMONG US TO BE ENLIGHTENED!
NO! RANGER! DON'T DO IT!
RRRRRRR--

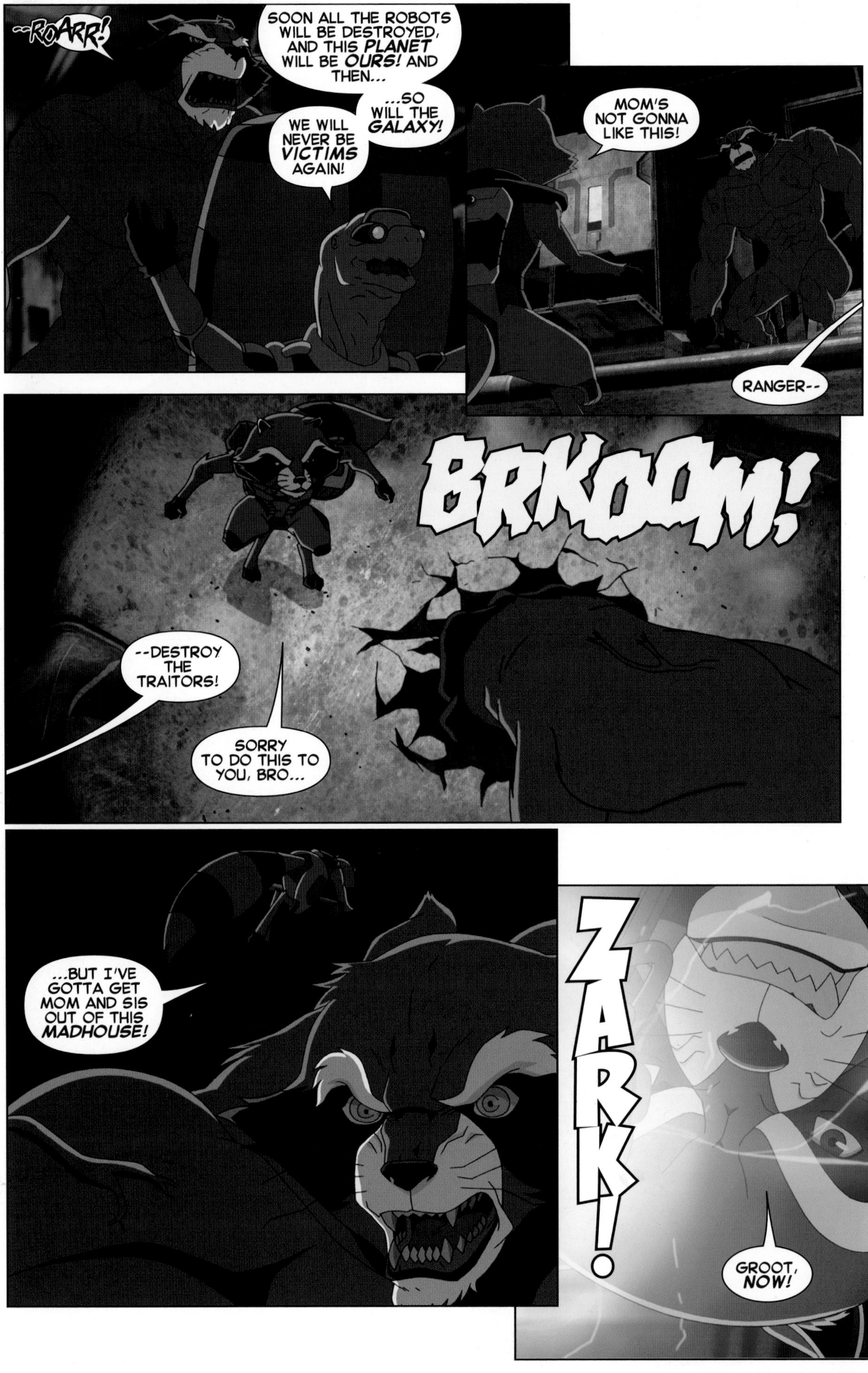
--ROARR!
SOON ALL THE ROBOTS WILL BE DESTROYED, AND THIS *PLANET* WILL BE *OURS!* AND THEN...
...SO WILL THE *GALAXY!*
WE WILL NEVER BE *VICTIMS* AGAIN!
MOM'S NOT GONNA LIKE THIS!
RANGER--
BRKOOM!
--DESTROY THE TRAITORS!
SORRY TO DO THIS TO YOU, BRO...
...BUT I'VE GOTTA GET MOM AND SIS OUT OF THIS *MADHOUSE!*
ZARK!
GROOT, *NOW!*

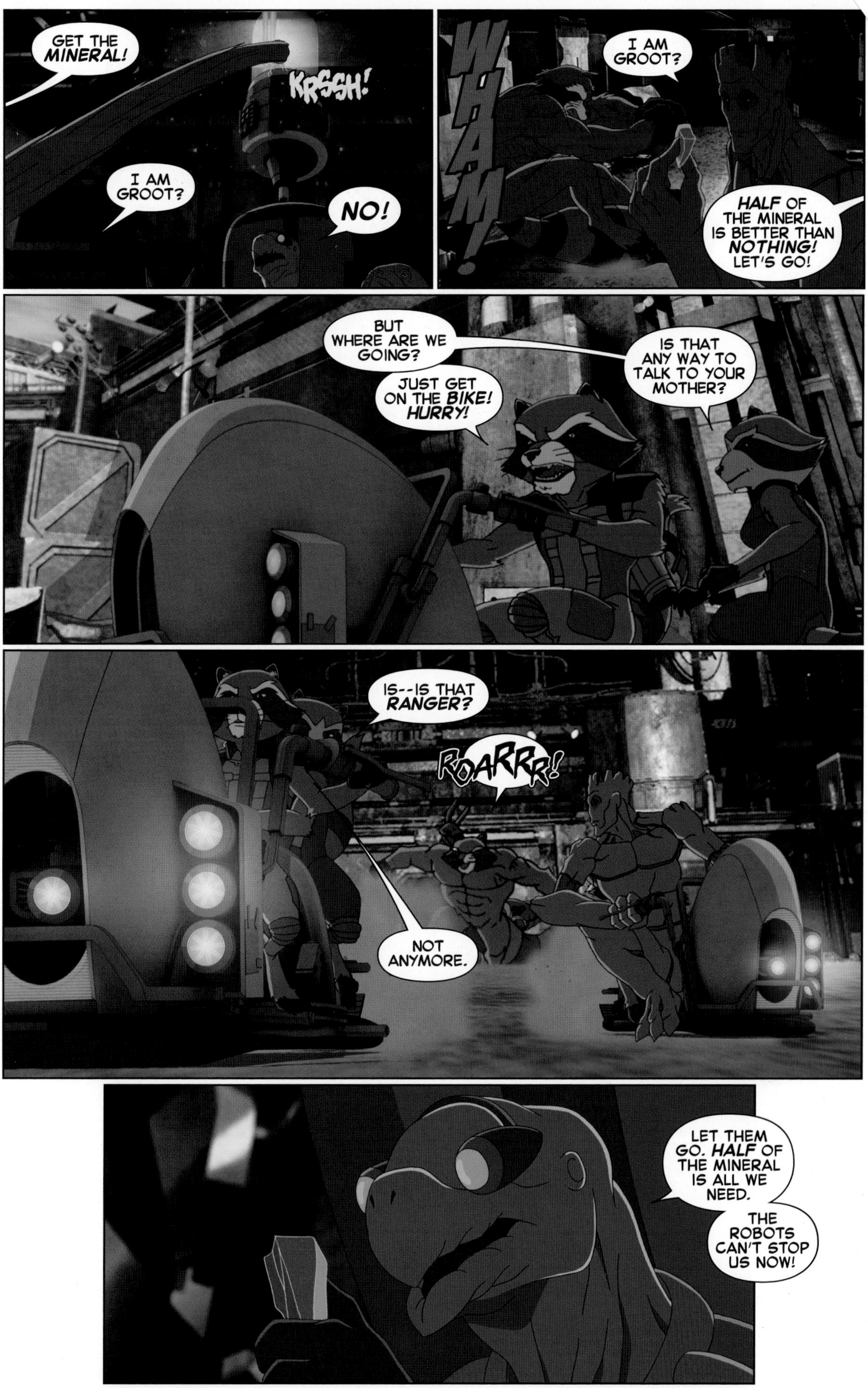
GET THE MINERAL!
KRSSH!
I AM GROOT?
NO!
WHAM!
I AM GROOT?
HALF OF THE MINERAL IS BETTER THAN NOTHING! LET'S GO!
BUT WHERE ARE WE GOING?
JUST GET ON THE BIKE! HURRY!
IS THAT ANY WAY TO TALK TO YOUR MOTHER?
IS--IS THAT RANGER?
ROARRR!
NOT ANYMORE.
LET THEM GO. HALF OF THE MINERAL IS ALL WE NEED.
THE ROBOTS CAN'T STOP US NOW!

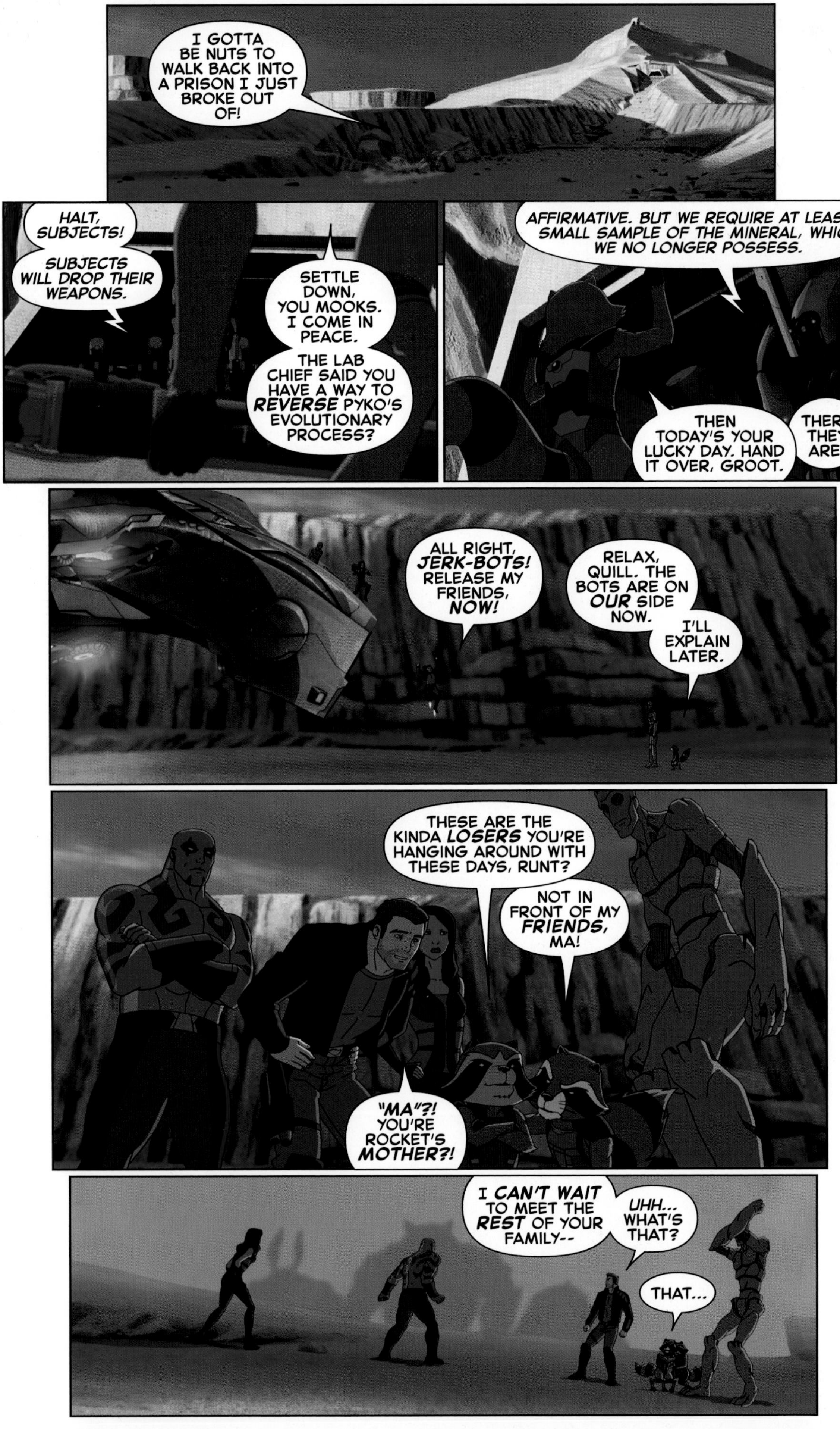

I GOTTA BE NUTS TO WALK BACK INTO A PRISON I JUST BROKE OUT OF!
HALT, SUBJECTS!
SUBJECTS WILL DROP THEIR WEAPONS.
SETTLE DOWN, YOU MOOKS. I COME IN PEACE.
THE LAB CHIEF SAID YOU HAVE A WAY TO REVERSE PYKO'S EVOLUTIONARY PROCESS?
AFFIRMATIVE. BUT WE REQUIRE AT LEAST A SMALL SAMPLE OF THE MINERAL, WHICH WE NO LONGER POSSESS.
THEN TODAY'S YOUR LUCKY DAY. HAND IT OVER, GROOT.
THERE THEY ARE!
ALL RIGHT, JERK-BOTS! RELEASE MY FRIENDS, NOW!
RELAX, QUILL. THE BOTS ARE ON OUR SIDE NOW.
I'LL EXPLAIN LATER.
THESE ARE THE KINDA LOSERS YOU'RE HANGING AROUND WITH THESE DAYS, RUNT?
NOT IN FRONT OF MY FRIENDS, MA!
"MA"?! YOU'RE ROCKET'S MOTHER?!
I CAN'T WAIT TO MEET THE REST OF YOUR FAMILY--
UHH... WHAT'S THAT?
THAT...

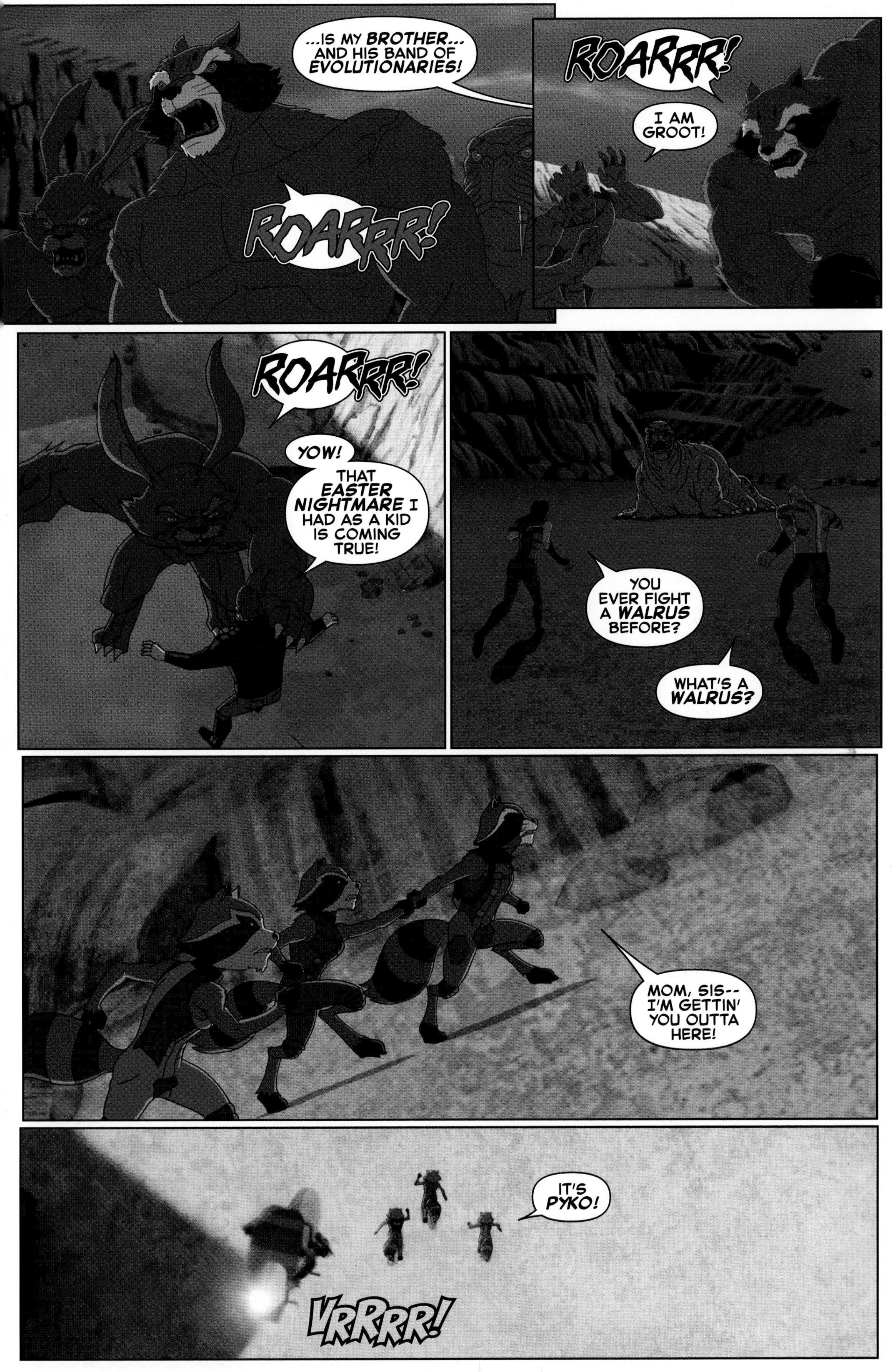
...IS MY BROTHER... AND HIS BAND OF EVOLUTIONARIES!
ROARRR!
ROARRR!
I AM GROOT!
ROARRR!
YOW!
THAT EASTER NIGHTMARE I HAD AS A KID IS COMING TRUE!
YOU EVER FIGHT A WALRUS BEFORE?
WHAT'S A WALRUS?
MOM, SIS-- I'M GETTIN' YOU OUTTA HERE!
IT'S PYKO!
VRRRR!

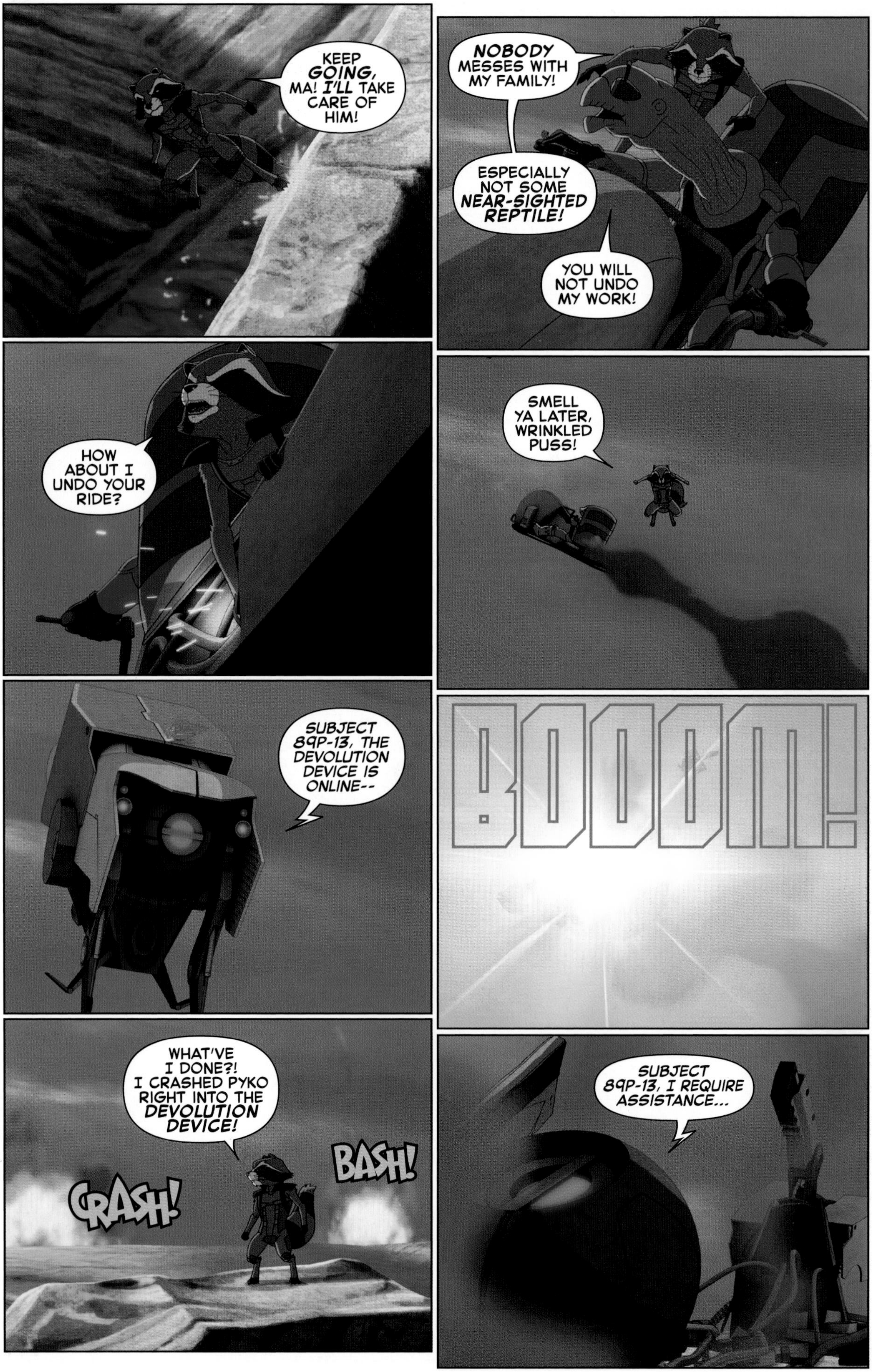
KEEP GOING, MA! I'LL TAKE CARE OF HIM!
NOBODY MESSES WITH MY FAMILY!
ESPECIALLY NOT SOME NEAR-SIGHTED REPTILE!
YOU WILL NOT UNDO MY WORK!
HOW ABOUT I UNDO YOUR RIDE?
SMELL YA LATER, WRINKLED PUSS!
SUBJECT 89P-13, THE DEVOLUTION DEVICE IS ONLINE--
BOOOM!
WHAT'VE I DONE?! I CRASHED PYKO RIGHT INTO THE DEVOLUTION DEVICE!
CRASH!
BASH!
SUBJECT 89P-13, I REQUIRE ASSISTANCE...

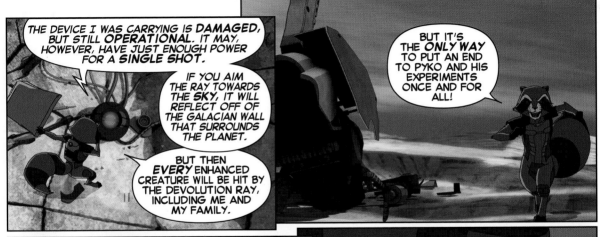

THE DEVICE I WAS CARRYING IS *DAMAGED*, BUT STILL *OPERATIONAL*. IT MAY, HOWEVER, HAVE JUST ENOUGH POWER FOR A *SINGLE SHOT*.

IF YOU AIM THE RAY TOWARDS THE *SKY*, IT WILL REFLECT OFF OF THE GALACIAN WALL THAT SURROUNDS THE PLANET.

BUT THEN *EVERY* ENHANCED CREATURE WILL BE HIT BY THE DEVOLUTION RAY, INCLUDING ME AND MY *FAMILY*.

BUT IT'S THE *ONLY WAY* TO PUT AN END TO PYKO AND HIS EXPERIMENTS ONCE AND FOR ALL!

NO!

HEY!

DON'T DO THIS! *JOIN* ME INSTEAD! TOGETHER WE CAN *RULE* THE GALAXY!

I'M NOT INTERESTED IN *RULING* THE GALAXY, YOU SHRIVELED-UP MANIAC!

I'M HERE TO *GUARD* IT!

TALKING AND WALKING UPRIGHT WAS FUN WHILE IT LASTED--

CLICK

--BUT I'VE GOT A *WORLD* TO SAVE!

VMMMM!

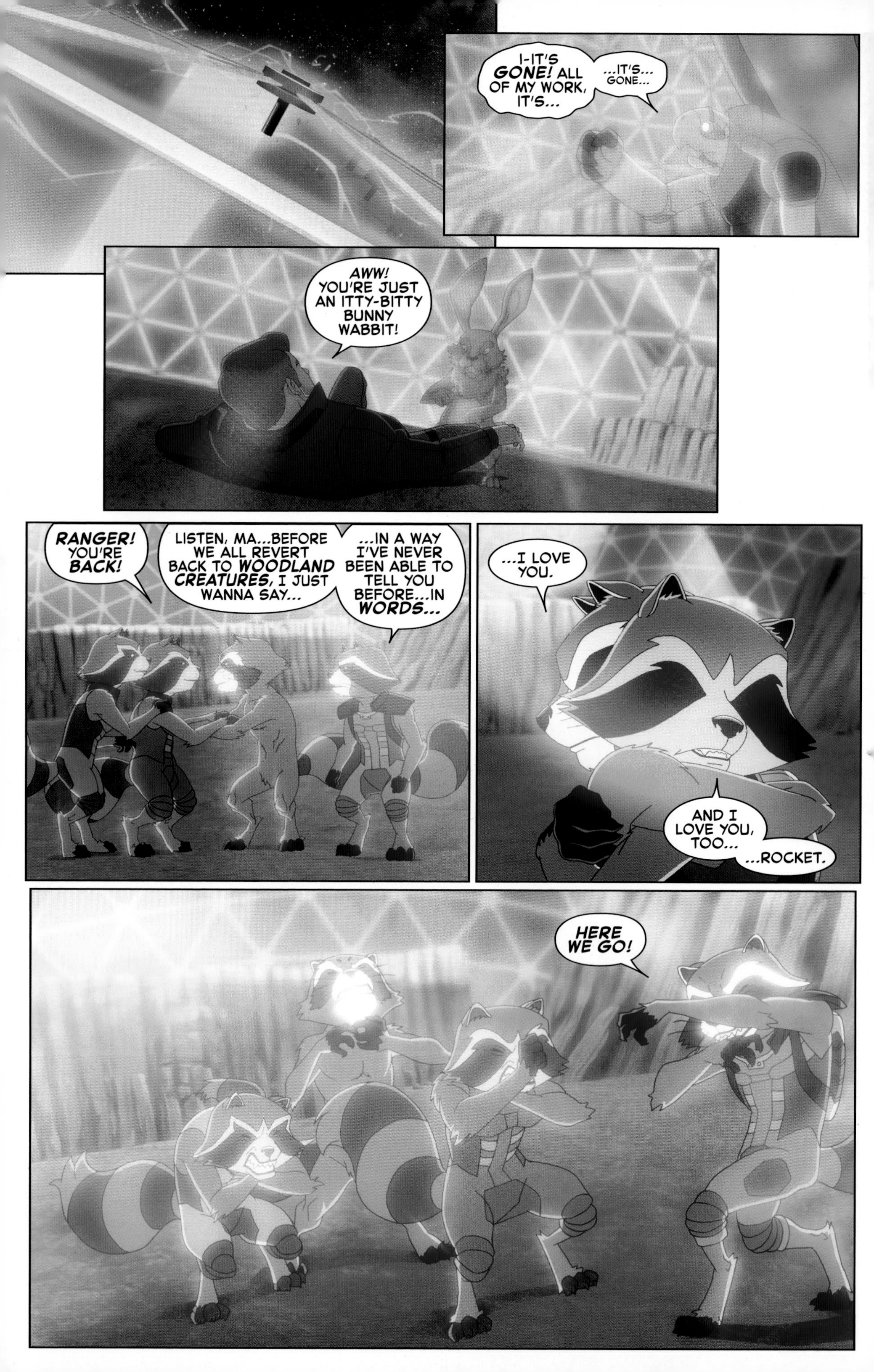
I-IT'S GONE! ALL OF MY WORK, IT'S...
...IT'S... GONE...
AWW! YOU'RE JUST AN ITTY-BITTY BUNNY WABBIT!
RANGER! YOU'RE BACK!
LISTEN, MA...BEFORE WE ALL REVERT BACK TO WOODLAND CREATURES, I JUST WANNA SAY...
...IN A WAY I'VE NEVER BEEN ABLE TO TELL YOU BEFORE...IN WORDS...
...I LOVE YOU.
AND I LOVE YOU, TOO...
...ROCKET.
HERE WE GO!

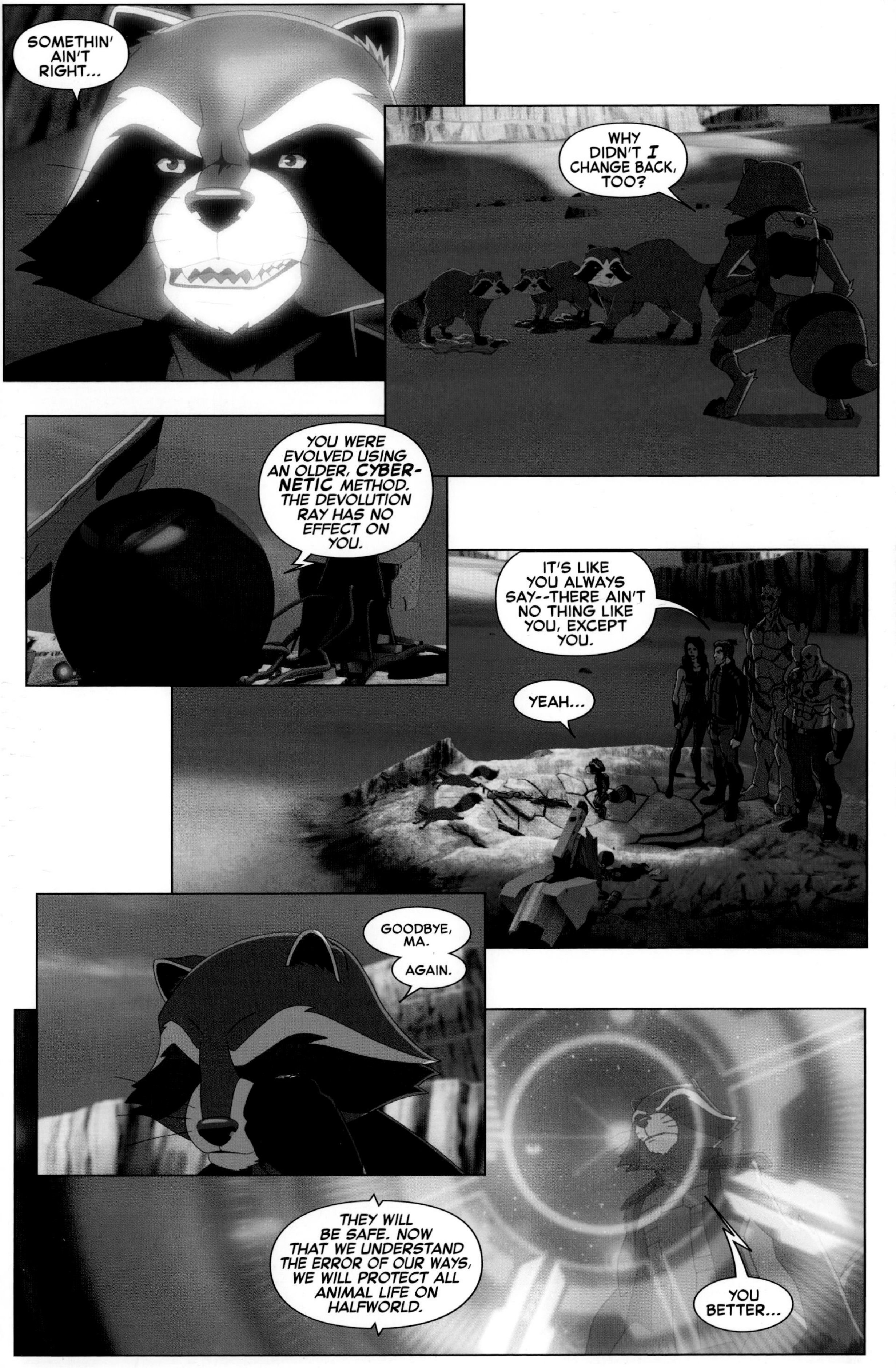
SOMETHIN' AIN'T RIGHT...
WHY DIDN'T I CHANGE BACK, TOO?
YOU WERE EVOLVED USING AN OLDER, CYBER-NETIC METHOD. THE DEVOLUTION RAY HAS NO EFFECT ON YOU.
IT'S LIKE YOU ALWAYS SAY--THERE AIN'T NO THING LIKE YOU, EXCEPT YOU.
YEAH...
GOODBYE, MA.
AGAIN.
THEY WILL BE SAFE. NOW THAT WE UNDERSTAND THE ERROR OF OUR WAYS, WE WILL PROTECT ALL ANIMAL LIFE ON HALFWORLD.
YOU BETTER...

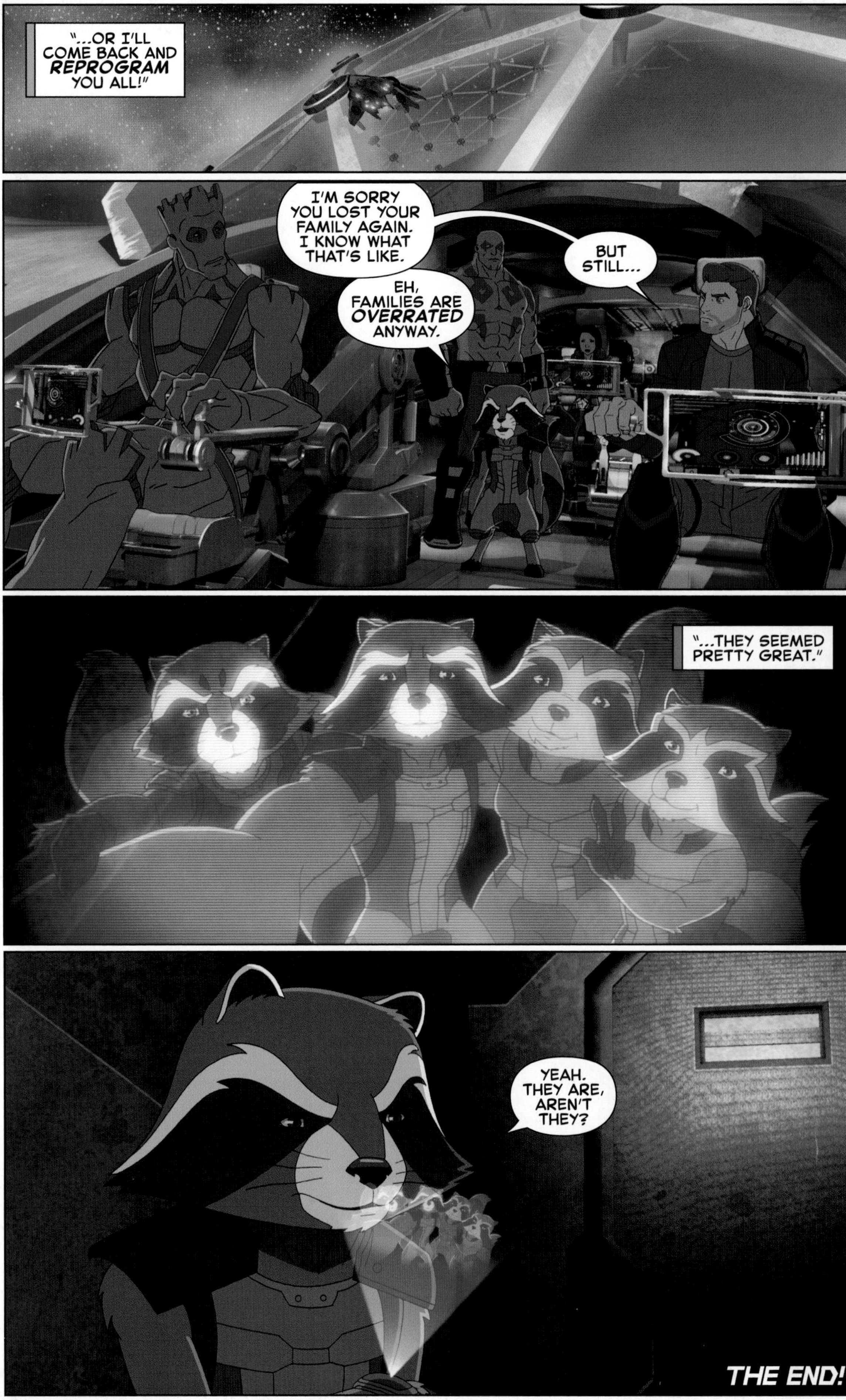
"...OR I'LL COME BACK AND **REPROGRAM** YOU ALL!"
I'M SORRY YOU LOST YOUR FAMILY AGAIN. I KNOW WHAT THAT'S LIKE.
BUT STILL...
EH, FAMILIES ARE **OVERRATED** ANYWAY.
"...THEY SEEMED PRETTY GREAT."
YEAH. THEY ARE, AREN'T THEY?
THE END!

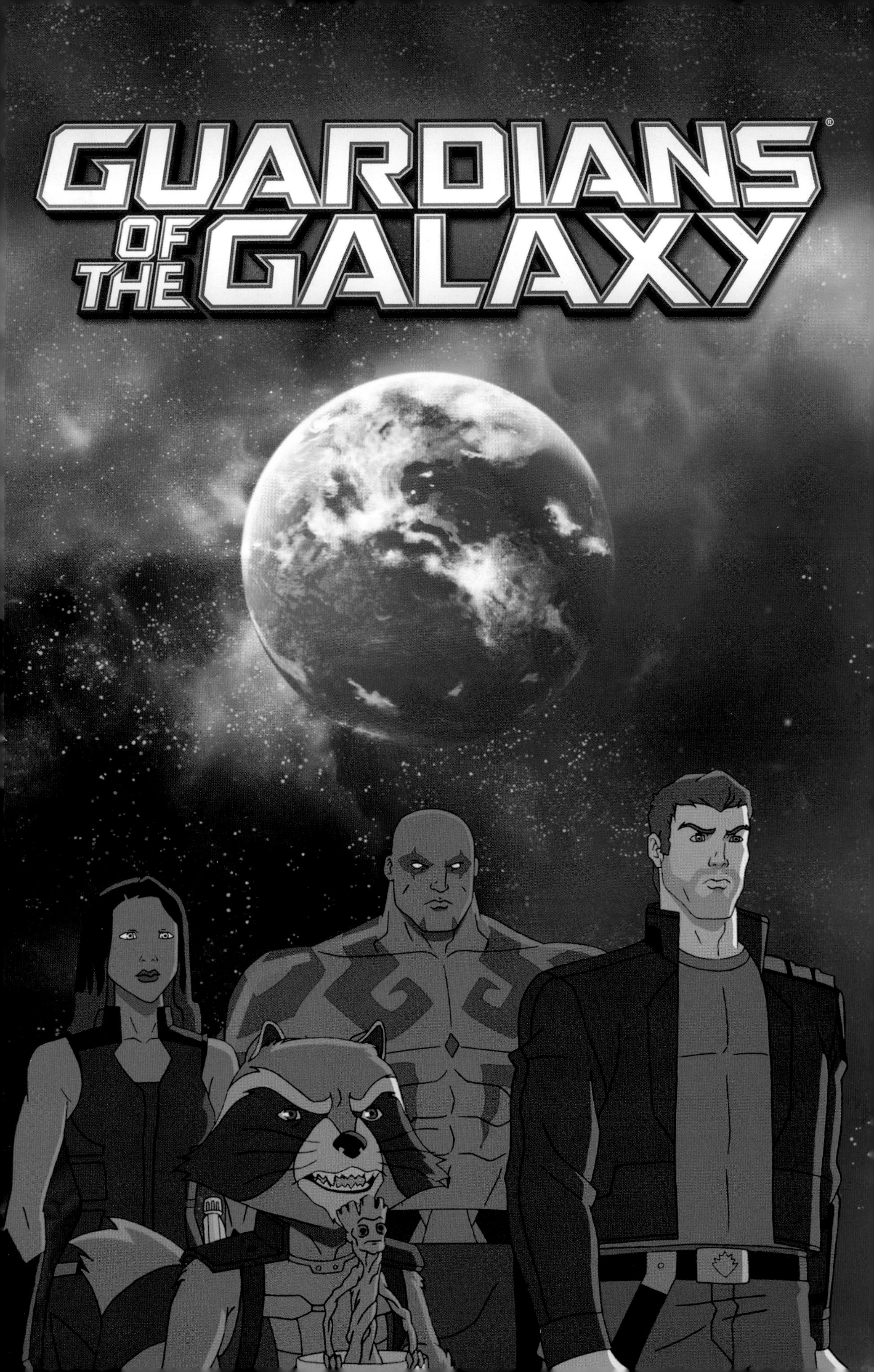
GUARDIANS
OF THE GALAXY

GUARDIANS OF THE GALAXY

COLLECT THEM ALL!

Set of 6 Hardcover Books ISBN: 978-1-5321-4357-1

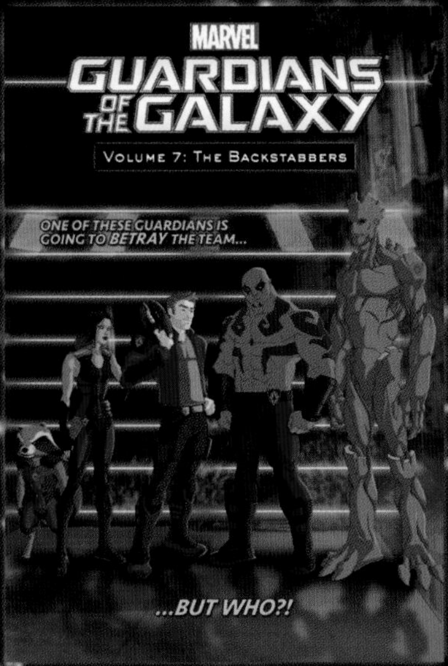
MARVEL
GUARDIANS OF THE GALAXY
VOLUME 7: THE BACKSTABBERS
ONE OF THESE GUARDIANS IS GOING TO BETRAY THE TEAM...
...BUT WHO?!

Hardcover Book ISBN
978-1-5321-4358-8

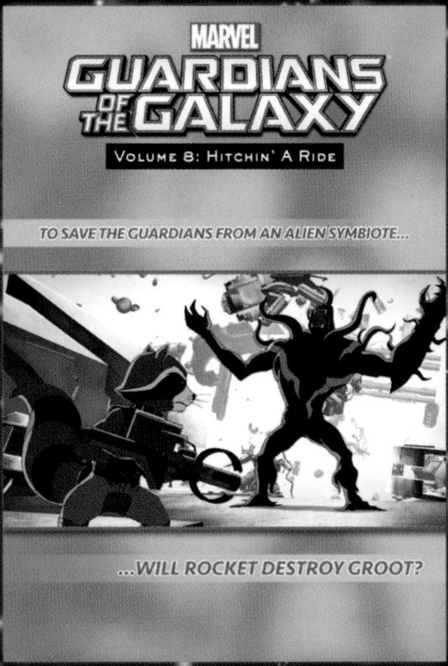
MARVEL
GUARDIANS OF THE GALAXY
VOLUME 8: HITCHIN' A RIDE
TO SAVE THE GUARDIANS FROM AN ALIEN SYMBIOTE...
...WILL ROCKET DESTROY GROOT?

Hardcover Book ISBN
978-1-5321-4359-5

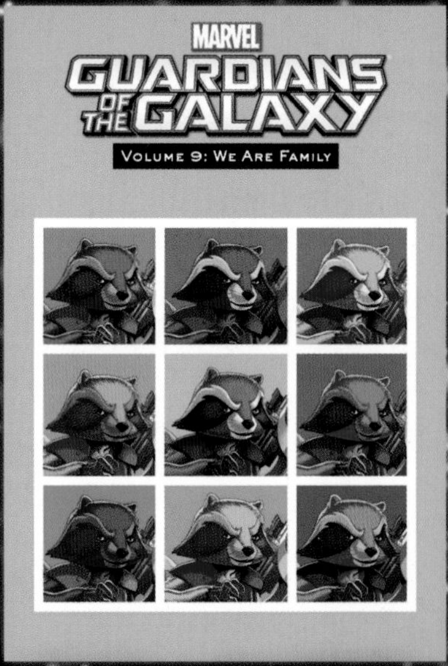
MARVEL
GUARDIANS OF THE GALAXY
VOLUME 9: WE ARE FAMILY

Hardcover Book ISBN
978-1-5321-4360-1

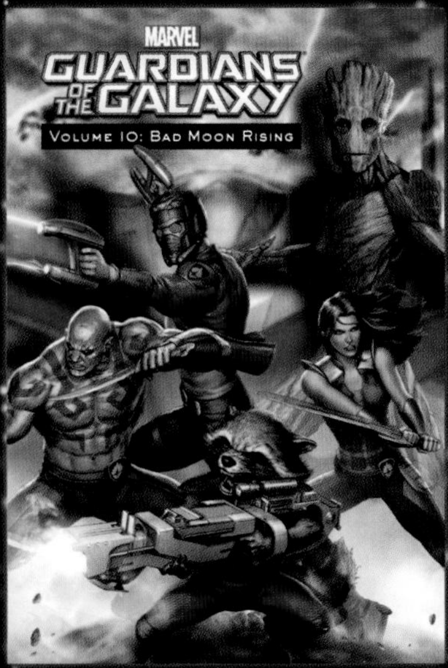
MARVEL
GUARDIANS OF THE GALAXY
VOLUME 10: BAD MOON RISING

Hardcover Book ISBN
978-1-5321-4361-8

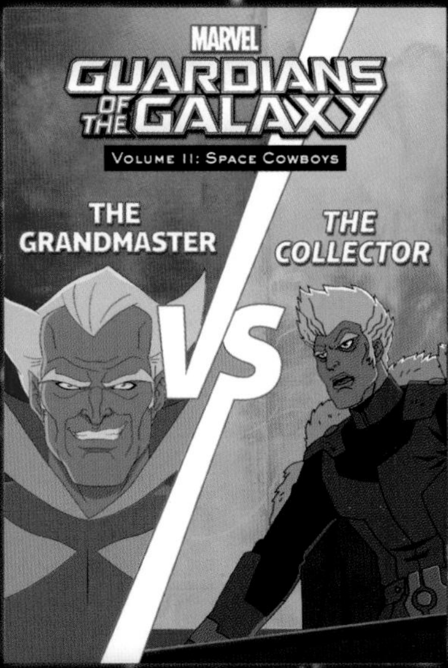
MARVEL
GUARDIANS OF THE GALAXY
VOLUME 11: SPACE COWBOYS
THE GRANDMASTER
VS
THE COLLECTOR

Hardcover Book ISBN
978-1-5321-4362-5

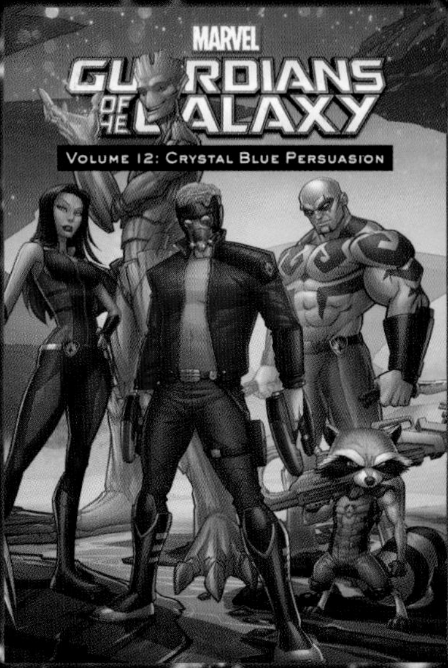
MARVEL
GUARDIANS OF THE GALAXY
VOLUME 12: CRYSTAL BLUE PERSUASION

Hardcover Book ISBN
978-1-5321-4363-2